Why Not?

by A. H. Benjamin

Illustrated by Tomislav Zlatic

W
FRANKLIN WATTS
LONDON•SYDNEY

Monkey sat high in the tree.
He saw Giraffe below him.

Cheekily, he slid down
her neck. "Don't do
that!" cried Giraffe.

"Why not?" laughed Monkey and he ran off.

Monkey had not gone far when he bumped into Elephant.

Monkey took hold of
Elephant's trunk and
blew into it.

"Don't do that!" bellowed
Elephant.

"Why not?" laughed
Monkey. Off he ran again.

Next he spotted Python
hanging from a branch.

12

13

Monkey crept up and
started to swing.

"Don't do that!"
gasped Python.
"Why not?" laughed
Monkey.

Then Monkey jumped
through the air and
landed on Hippo's back.

Monkey began to bounce.

"Don't do that!" snorted Hippo. "Why not?" laughed Monkey.

Finally, Monkey came to the river and began to drink.

He did not hear Crocodile
crawling behind him.

When Crocodile was right
behind Monkey, he opened
his huge mouth and went ...

23

Snap!

25

This scared Monkey so much that he jumped up and splashed head first into the river.

27

When Monkey bobbed up, Crocodile had a huge grin on his face.

"DON'T DO THAT!"
shrieked Monkey.

29

"Why not?" laughed Crocodile.

31

Leapfrog has been specially designed to fit the requirements of the National Literacy Strategy. It offers real books for beginning readers by top authors and illustrators. There are 67 Leapfrog stories to choose from:

* hardback